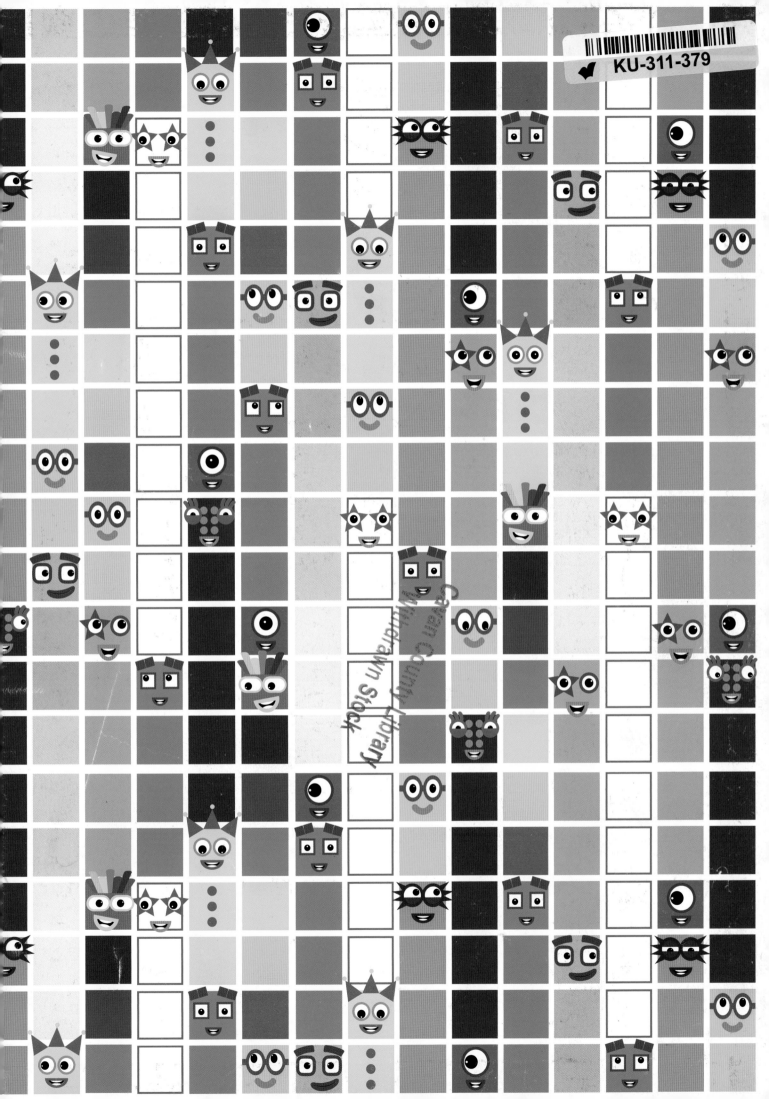

THIS BOOK
BELONGS TO

_ _ _ _ _ _ _ _ _ _ _

Published by Sweet Cherry Publishing Limited
Unit 36, Vulcan House,
Vulcan Road,
Leicester, LE5 3EF
United Kingdom

Published in 2019

2 4 6 8 10 9 7 5 3 1

ISBN: 978-1-78226-595-5

Written by Jasmine Allen

www.sweetcherrypublishing.com

Printed and manufactured in Turkey
T.I O006

ANNUAL 2020

CONTENTS

MEET NUMBERBLOCK ONE

> I am Numberblock One. **This is fun!**

FACT FILE

- She loves to find things that are **on their own**.

- She has **one big round eye**.

- She cannot change shape like the other Numberblocks, because she is only **one block**.

> Can you find **one** thing in your house that is red?

One Big Adventure

Can you help Numberblock One find a path through the maze to reach the apple?

Make sure I don't get stuck anywhere!

START

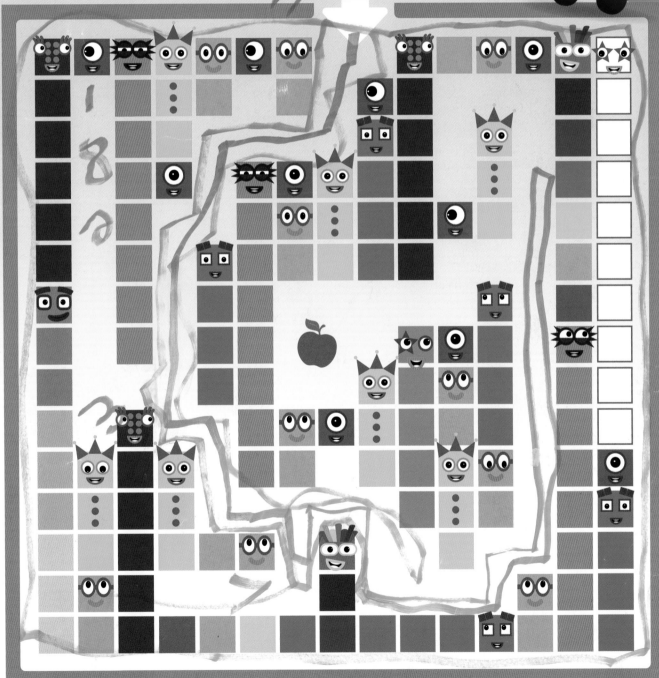

ONE HAS FUN!

1

Numberblock One is in Numberland!

2

One goes exploring. She finds **one** bird.

3

The bird flies away. She follows it and finds **one** big tree.

4

One finds more animals near the tree. She sees **one** buzzing bee ...

5

... and **one** tiny ant!

6

One looks up to the sky. She sees **one** very big round thing. It's the sun!

7

Then **One** goes on a boat. She sees **one** big blue whale.

8

One has found lots of things, but she still feels sad. She wishes there were more **Numberblocks** in Numberland.

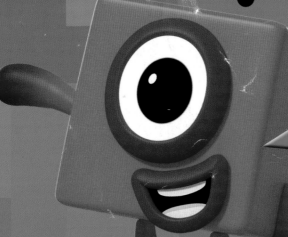

Go to page 14 to see me make a friend!

11

ONE'S WONDERFUL WORLD

Numberblock One loves finding one of things. What can you find in this scene? Colour them in as you go!

12

TWO FOR TENNIS

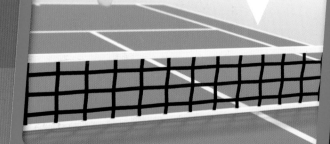

1

Numberblock One wants to play tennis. She finds **one** tennis racket and **one** tennis ball.

2

She hits the ball over the net. But no one is there to hit the ball back.

3

This makes **Numberblock One** sad. She wishes that she had a **Numberblock friend** to play with.

4

Numberblock One finds a magic mirror. It helps her make another **One** ... and another **One!**

5

Now there are three **One** blocks! **One** jumps on top of another **One.**

6

This makes **Numberblock Two**. **One** and **Two** are very happy to meet each other.

7

They go to the tennis court. **Numberblock Two** has **two** tennis rackets.

8

Numberblock One and **Numberblock Two** play tennis. They become **best friends**.

Go to
page 22
to see Three's
magic trick!

MEET NUMBERBLOCK TWO

2

I am Numberblock Two. **How do you do?**

I love dancing in my **two** dancing shoes !

Can you find two **matching** things in your house?

FACT FILE

- He has **two** shoes, **two** socks and **two** blocks.

- He loves **making pairs** of things.

- He is **Numberblock One's** best friend.

I Spy a Pair

Two things that go together are called a pair. Find the pairs on this page and draw a line to connect them.

I can look like this, too!

2

2

Everything is better with two !

TEATIME TREASURE HUNT

Numberblocks One and Two are enjoying some tasty tea and cake. Can you find the parts of the picture that are in the close-ups?

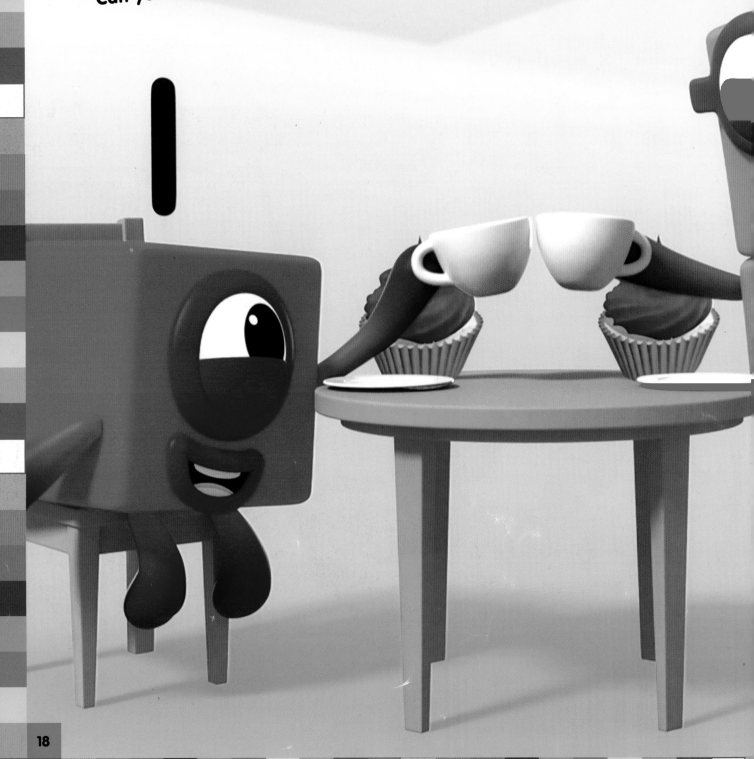

2

Take a closer look!

1

A

B

C

D

2

Did you find them all?

Check your answers on page 66.

MEET NUMBERBLOCK THREE

3

I am Numberblock Three. **Look at me!**

I juggle **three** balls. Can you juggle?

3

FACT FILE

- She loves to make people **smile** and **laugh**.

- She wears a big **red crown** with **three** triangles on it.

- She thinks she is the best **Numberblock**.

Silly Threes

Numberblock Three has been dressing up in very silly outfits! Can you spot the Three below who is not dressed up?

I am one block away from being a square!

3

A

B

C

D

E

Do you like to play fancy dress?

3

Check your answers on page 66.

THREE'S TASTY TRICK

1

Numberblock Three is doing cartwheels. She picks **three** apples off the tree.

2

Let's play a game! She takes the **three** apples over to a table with **three** cups.

3

She hides **one** apple under **one** of the cups.

4

Three moves the cups around and around. Then, **One** and **Two** have to guess where the apple is.

5

One thinks the apple is under the **red** cup ... but it is not.

6

Two thinks the apple is under the **orange** cup ... but it is not.

7

The apple was under the **yellow** cup all along!

8

Time to **eat** some apples!

Go to page 28 to see Four's adventure in Flatland.

PUT ON A SHOW!

Numberblocks One, Two and Three are putting on a show! Can you find all the things that are hidden on the stage?
Tick them off once you have found them.

3

1 BOAT

2 TREES

3 BALL

MEET NUMBERBLOCK FOUR

4

I am Numberblock Four. **I love squares!**

I like all things with **four** sides!

I can also stand up **tall**, like this.

4

FACT FILE

- **Four** is made of **squares**. Even his eyes and eyebrows are made out of **squares!**

- He does not like **round** things.

- He has a fluffy brown pet called **Squarey!** Can you spot her?

Small to Tall

The Numberblocks are sorting themselves from smallest to biggest. Which sequence is right?

A

B

C

D

Am I standing in the **correct** place?

Check your answers on page 66.

FOUR GOES TO FLATLAND

1

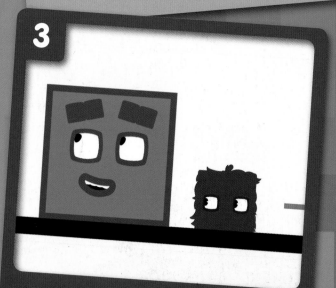

Numberblock Four is playing with his pet, **Squarey**. He throws a stick for **Squarey** to fetch.

2

The stick gets stuck in a wall. **Squarey** jumps after it. She gets stuck too!

3

Four follows **Squarey**. They are in Flatland! **Four** is now a flat 2D shape with **four** equal sides ... he's a **square**!

4

Four and **Squarey** meet a shape with **three** sides. It's a **triangle**. Lots of little **triangles** fit together to make one big **triangle**!

5

They meet lots of shapes with **four** sides, too. They are not **squares** because their sides are not **equal**.

6

Two new shapes come along. They make a hot-air balloon for **Four** and **Squarey** to sit in.

7

The hot-air balloon flies up and up ... and throws them back into **Numberland**!

8

Four and **Squarey** are not flat anymore!

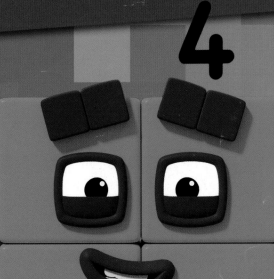

Go to page 34 to see me playing hide-and-seek!

STAMP FUN!

Numberblock Four loves playing with paint! He turns into lots of different shapes and stamps himself on the wall. Can you match his different shapes with the stamps he made?

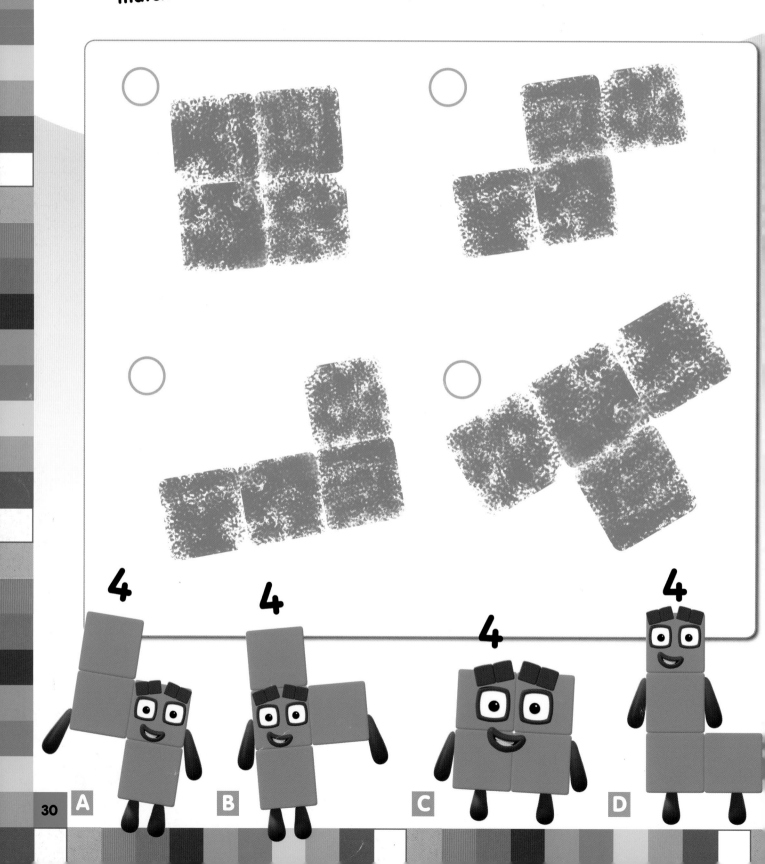

A   B   C   D

MEET NUMBERBLOCK FIVE

5

5

I can look like steps!

I am Numberblock Five. **High five!**

FACT FILE

- She loves to **high five** people with her **big blue hand**.

- One of her eyes is a **star**.

- She loves to **sing** with her microphone.

True or False

How well do you know the Numberblocks?
Read each sentences below. Draw a tick if a
sentence is true. Draw a cross if it is false.

Did you
get all five
correct?

**Numberblock One
is orange.** ◯

**Numberblock Two
loves to dance.** ◯

**Numberblock Three
has five buttons down
her front.** ◯

**Numberblock Four has
a pet called Squarey.** ◯

**Numberblock Five is
very shy.** ◯

Check your answers on page 66. **33**

FIVE'S FUN GAME!

Numberblocks One, Two, Three and **Four** ask **Five** to play hide-and-seek with them.

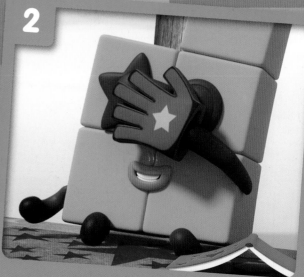

Five covers her eyes and counts to **five**. The other **Numberblocks** run away to hide.

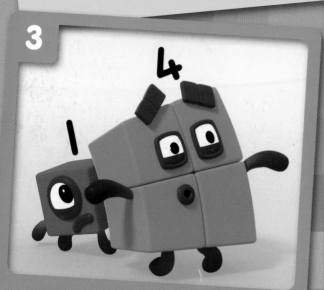

One and **Four** are looking for somewhere to hide. **Whoops!** They bump into each other.

This makes another **Numberblock Five!**

5

The new **Numberblock Five** puts handprints on the tree. They show where **Four** and **One** will go.

6

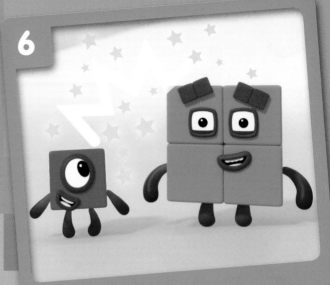

Naughty **Numberblock Five** turns back into **One** and **Four**.

7

One and **Four** see the handprints on the tree and run the other way. They cannot be **tricked**!

8

One and **Four** hide, and **Five** cannot find them. They **win** the game!

5

Go to page 40 to read about the cheeky sheep that will not sleep!

ALL ABOUT THE NUMBERBLOCKS!

Can you answer these questions?

A. Who has the most blocks?

B. Whose favourite shape is a square?

C. Who likes to dance?

D. Who has one big round eye?

E. Who can juggle?

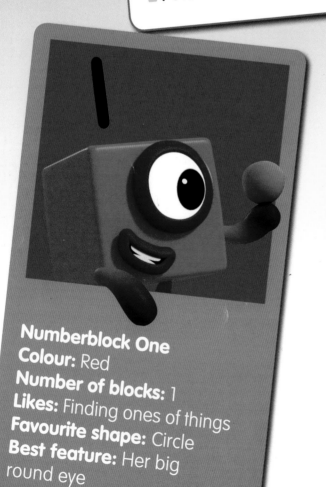

Numberblock One
Colour: Red
Number of blocks: 1
Likes: Finding ones of things
Favourite shape: Circle
Best feature: Her big round eye

Numberblock Two
Colour: Orange
Number of blocks: 2
Likes: Dancing
Favourite shape: Rectangle
Best feature: His dancing shoes

3

Numberblock Three
Colour: Yellow
Number of blocks: 3
Likes: Juggling
Favourite shape: Triangle
Best feature: Her beautiful red crown

4

Numberblock Four
Colour: Green
Number of blocks: 4
Likes: Playing with Squarey
Favourite shape: Square
Best feature: His funny square eyebrows

5

5

Numberblock Five
Colour: Blue
Number of blocks: 5
Likes: Singing and giving high fives
Favourite shape: Star
Best feature: Her big blue hand

MEET NUMBERBLOCK SIX

6

I am Numberblock Six. **Let's roll!**

6

I can be really **tall** ...

... or really **short** !

6

FACT FILE

- Six has **six** eyelashes. Can you count them all?

- She loves playing **games** with her friends.

- She likes to **rap,** and often speaks in **rhymes**.

6

Dotty Match

Draw in the missing domino dots! The dots on each tile must match the dots on the domino next to it.

Colour in the dominoes when you are finished!

6

How many 6s can you see? When you see a 6, think of me!

6

SIX CHEEKY SHEEP

2

Counting the sheep makes **Six** fall asleep. While she sleeps, the sheep sneak away.

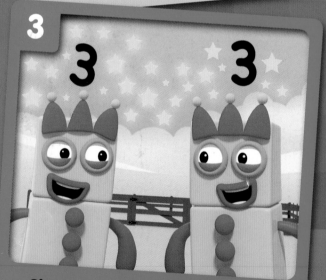

1

Numberblock Six is putting **six** sheep into their pen. It's time for bed.

3

Six wakes up. She splits into **two Numberblock Threes** to round up the sheep.

4

But catching the sheep is very tricky! So **Six** splits into **three Numberblock Twos.**

5

But they still cannot catch all the sheep. **Six** splits into **six Numberblock Ones**.

6

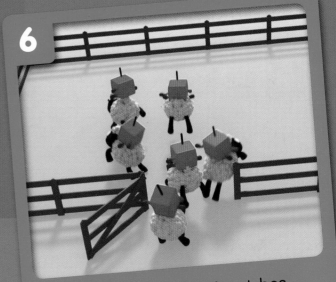

Each **Numberblock** catches **one** sheep. They ride the sheep back into the pen.

7

If counting sheep sends **Numberblocks** to sleep, maybe counting **Numberblocks** sends sheep to sleep!

8

It works! All **six** sheep fall asleep.

Go to **page 46** to join us on our rainy-day picnic.

BLOCKS AND LADDERS

START

Take it in turns to roll the dice. Move your counter the amount of spaces shown on the dice. If you land on an instruction square, do what it says!

Move back 2 spaces

Miss a turn

Take a shortcut

Move forwards 2 spaces

Move back 1+1 spaces

5

Take a shortcut

3

Move back 2+1 spaces

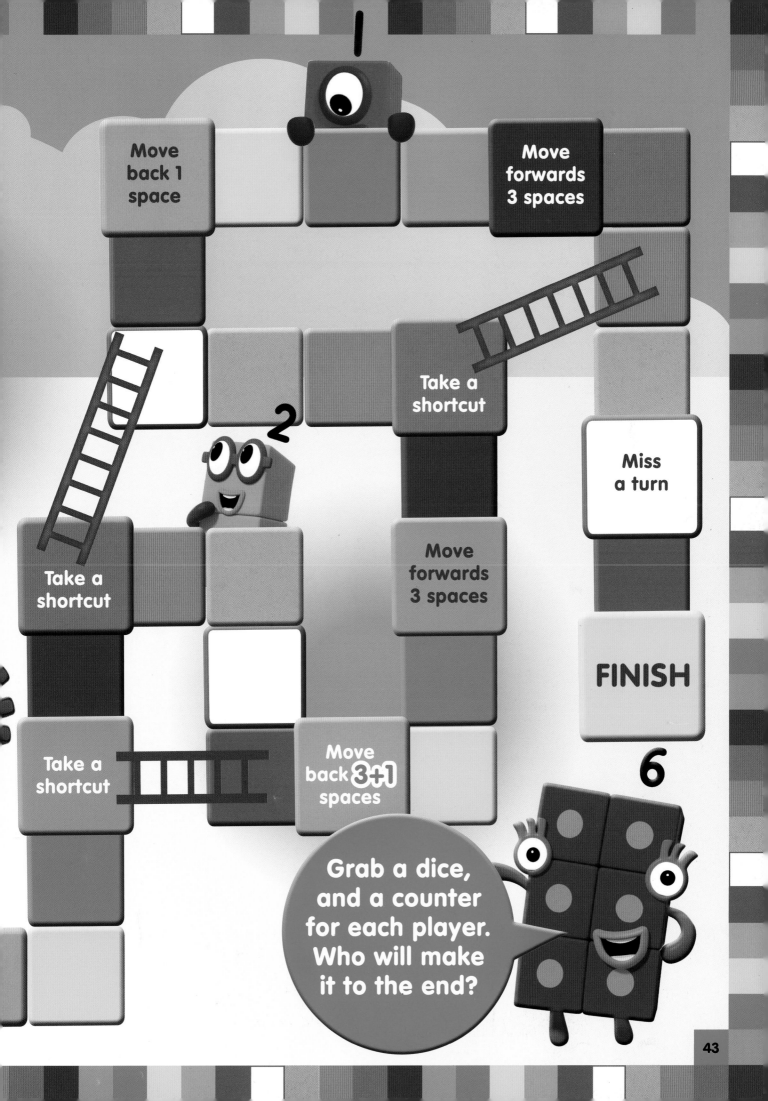

MEET NUMBERBLOCK SEVEN

7

I am Numberblock Seven. **I am very lucky!**

I can be lots of shapes.

7

7

FACT FILE

- His blocks are the colours of the **rainbow**.

- Seven has spiky **rainbow-coloured** hair.

- He can make **rainbows** appear from his blocks!

Find the Path

Follow the sequence at the bottom of the page to help Seven find a path to his friends!

7

Sequence

A VERY WET PICNIC

1

One sunny day **Numberblocks One**, **Two**, **Three**, **Four**, **Five** and **Six** are having a picnic.

2

Suddenly, a big grey cloud appears. Rain starts pouring down.

3

One finds an umbrella. She stands on everyone's heads to keep them dry, starting with **Two**, then **Three**, then **Four**.

4

But when she jumps onto **Five**, she starts to wobble ...

5

... and falls straight onto **Six**.

6

One and **Six** join together to make **Numberblock Seven**!

7

Then a beautiful **rainbow** appears in the sky. **Seven's** blocks turn the colours of the rainbow.

8

Now the sun is shining! The **Numberblocks** go back to their picnic.

Go to page 52 to see Octoblock save the day!

NUMBERBLOCK SWAPS

Look carefully at these two scenes. Can you spot the differences?

Each time you find a difference, draw a tick in one of the circles opposite!

1

2

3

4

5

6

1

MEET NUMBERBLOCK EIGHT

8

I am Numberblock Eight. I am very brave!

8

I am also known as Octoblock!

FACT FILE

- He loves to wear his mask. It has **eight** points on it.

- He has **eight** tentacles. He uses them to climb, run, crawl and **tickle** his friends!

- He is always ready to help his friends.

Shadow Match

Match the Numberblocks to their shadows! Write the correct letter next to each Numberblock picture.

Did you match them all?

8

Check your answers on page 66.

OCTOBLOCK
TO THE RESCUE!

1

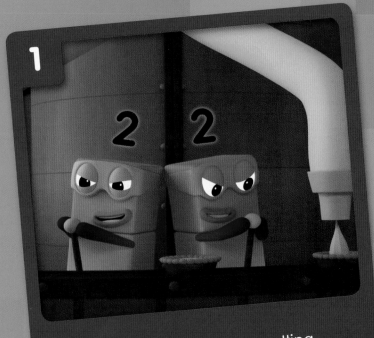

The **Terrible Twos** are getting into **trouble** again.

2

Here comes **Octoblock!**

3

Octoblock's Numberblock friends come to help him.

4

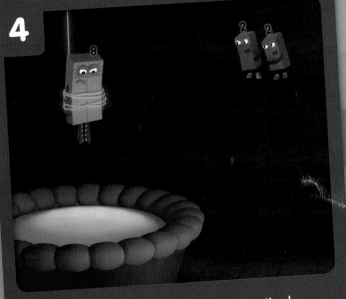

But the **Terrible Twos** have tied **Octoblock** up. He is hanging over a huge pie!

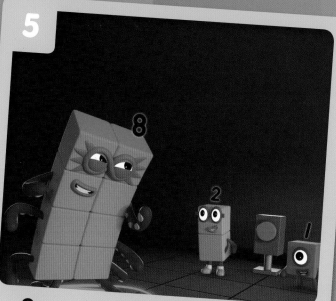

5

One and **Two** press a button to free **Octoblock**. The others circle around the **Terrible Twos**.

6

The **Terrible Twos** use the magic mirror to make more **Twos**.

7

Four **Terrible Twos** make one **Octonaughty**! **Octonaughty** tries to run away ...

8

Cheeky **Octonaughty** falls right into the pie!

Go to **page 58** to read about One's fantastic photoshoot!

EIGHT IN EIGHT STEPS

Follow the instructions to draw Numberblock Eight!

1. Blocks

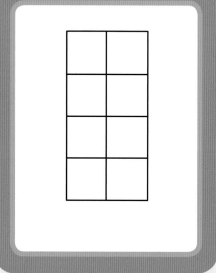

1 Draw his 8 blocks.

2. Tentacles

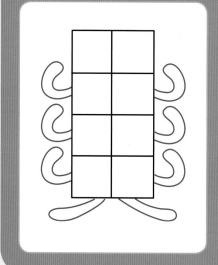

2 Draw 8 tentacles, 3 on each side and 2 at the bottom.

3. Suckers

3 Draw 4 spots on each tentacle.

5. Spikes

5 Draw 8 spikes on his mask, 4 on each side.

6. Eyes

6 Draw his eyes.

7. Mouth

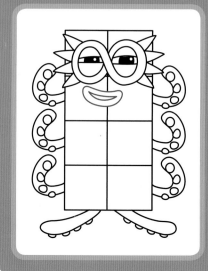

7 Draw on his smile.

Draw me in this space!

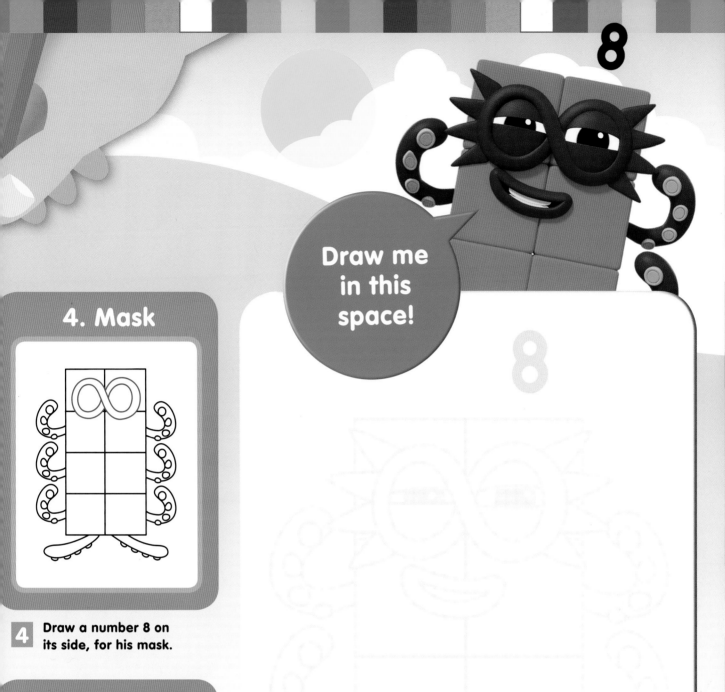

4. Mask

4 Draw a number 8 on its side, for his mask.

8. Colour

8 Colour Eight in with your favourite pens.

MEET NUMBERBLOCK NINE

9

I am Numberblock Nine. **Pleased to meet you!**

9

I can look like this, as well!

FACT FILE

- **Nine** is a **square**, just like Numberblock Four!

- **Achoo!!** Whenever he sneezes, he loses one of his blocks.

- He is made of **three** lots of **three blocks**.

56

Who Said That?

Read the sentences below and match them to the correct Numberblock.

'I'm one of a kind.'

'I'm the best of all the Numberblocks!'

'Blast off!'

'High Five!'

'I'll always be your friend.'

'Octoblock tickle!'

'Squares are strong.'

'Has anyone got a hanky?'

'I see a penny and I pick it up, and all day long I have good luck.'

9

'There's always time for one more game.'

Check your answers on page 66.

A HICCUPY PHOTOSHOOT

1

Numberblock One has a new camera. She wants to take pictures of **all** her Numberblock friends.

2

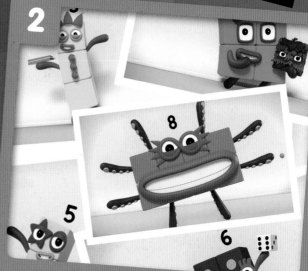

The **Numberblocks** take it in turns to have their picture taken. **Eight** pulls a funny face.

3

Next it is **Nine**'s turn. But Nine has the **hiccups**!

4

Every time **Nine** hiccups his blocks break apart into **smaller Numberblocks**!

5

Ten gives **Nine** some water. She tells him to drink it upside down ... but he just gets **wet**!

6

Octoblock says 'Boo!' to cure **Nine's** hiccups. But **Nine** jumps and turns into nine **Ones**!

7

Suddenly, the camera **explodes** from taking too many pictures.

8

Nine is so **shocked** that he stops hiccuping! **Hurray!**

Turn to page 64 to see who wins the Numberblock Rally!

COLLECT THE NUMBERBLOCKS!

Be the first player to collect five of the Numberblocks!

1. Take it in turns to roll the dice and move your counter around the circle.
2. Whenever you land on a new character, tick them off your list.
3. Keep going around the board. The first player to collect five different Numberblocks wins the game!

START

To play, you will need pencils, a dice, and a counter for each player.

MOVE AROUND THE CIRCLE UNTIL YOU HAVE COLLECTED THEM ALL!

	1
	2
	3
	4
	5
	6
	7
	8
	9

	1
	2
	3
	4
	5
	6
	7
	8
	9

3

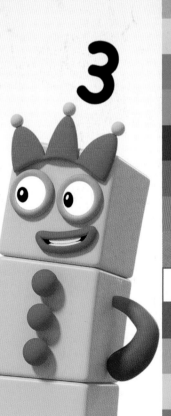

MEET NUMBERBLOCK TEN

10

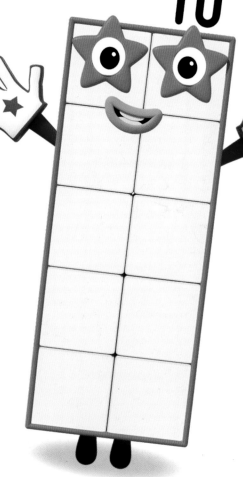

I am Numberblock Ten. 10 9 8 7 6 5 4 3 2 1 ...Blast off!

10

FACT FILE

- She can turn herself into a **rocket** and fly into space!

- Her eyes are red stars. Each star has **five** points. That is **ten** in total.

- She has two big hands, like **Numberblock Five's** big hand.

Count to Ten!

Join up the dots to draw Numberblock 10.

Start at 1 and draw up the steps!

THE NUMBERBLOCK RALLY

1

Numberblocks **Two** to **Ten** line up to have a race. Get set ... **GO!**

2

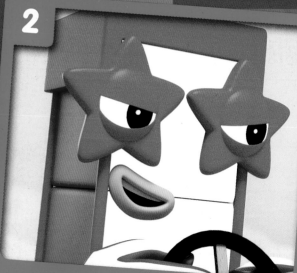

Ten really wants to win. She is the **biggest Numberblock** in the race, after all!

3

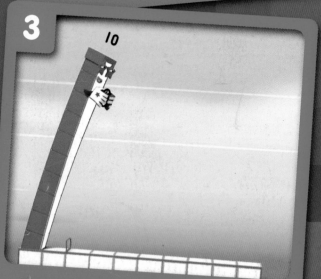

Ten whizzes into the lead. But she hits a **bump** and one of her blocks **falls off!**

4

With one less block, **Ten** becomes **Nine**.

5

The rest of the **Numberblocks** keep on racing. They try to catch up before the finish line.

6

CRASH! All of the Numberblocks bump into each other. Blocks go flying **everywhere**!

7

This leaves lots of **Numberblock Ones** racing towards the finish line.

8

Numberblock One wins the race!

All the **bigger** numbers are made up of Ones, so it's only fair that **One** should win!

ANSWERS

Page 9:

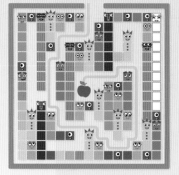

Page 17:

Page 18-19:

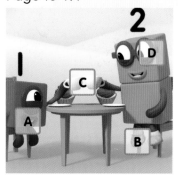

Page 21: It's E!

Page 24:

Page 27: It's C!

Page 30:

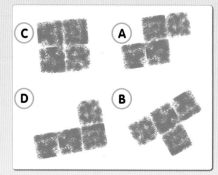

Page 33:
1 - False, 2 - True, 3 - False
4 - True, 5 - False

Page 36:
A - 5, B - 4, C - 2
D - 1, E - 3

Page 39:

Page 45:

Page 49:

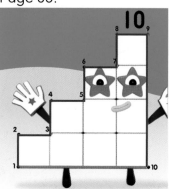

Page 51:

Page 57:
'I'm one of a kind.': **Numberblock One**
'I'm the best of all the Numberblocks!':
Numberblock Three
'Blast off!': **Numberblock Ten**
'I'll always be your friend.': **Numberblock Two**
'High Five': **Numberblock Five**
'Octoblock tickle!': **Numberblock Eight**
'Squares are strong.': **Numberblock Four**
'Has anyone got a hanky?': **Numberblock Nine**
'I see a penny and I pick it up, and all day long I
have good luck.': **Numberblock Seven**
'There's always time for one more game.':
Numberblock Six

Page 63:

PARENT'S GUIDE

Here are some great ways to get your children excited about numbers:

- Play a **'One says'** game with your child. Shout out 'One says…' and then follow it with an activity. 'One says do one jump!', 'One says give one hug!' etc.

- When you're out and about, keep an eye out for the **numbers**. While shopping: 'Can you find **two** apples?' While playing: 'Can you find **one** ball?' Also, ask them how many of certain things there are, e.g. '**How many** wheels are on the car?'

- Cut out cubes from old sponges so your child can make their own **Numberblock prints**, like in *Stamp Fun*. Explain that the more squares you have, the more shapes you will be able to make. **How many** shapes can the child make with four squares?

- Write numbers and include deliberate mistakes for your child to spot, e.g. **switching two numbers** around in a sequence (1, 2, 3, 5, 4, 6), writing a number back to front, writing an S instead of a 5, etc.

- While reading this annual ask your child questions about **what would happen** if certain characters joined together, or broke apart, or stood next to each other, etc. Use words like bigger/smaller, more/less, first/second/last, left/right or top/bottom/middle.

- Ask your child to **act like a Numberblock**! To be **Two**, march around counting steps; one, two, one, two. To be **Three**, play with three balls. To be **Four**, collect four things to put in a square. To be **Five**, count on your fingers then share a high five.

- **Make your own Numberblocks** with your child. Use any sort of blocks you have, and stick faces on them. See if your child can line them up in order, and ask them what happens when one jumps on top of another.

- **Roll two dice**. Then ask your child to identify the number of dots on the dice, and which character they match up with. Ask your child which dice shows more or fewer dots.

We hope you had fun with the

10

8

9

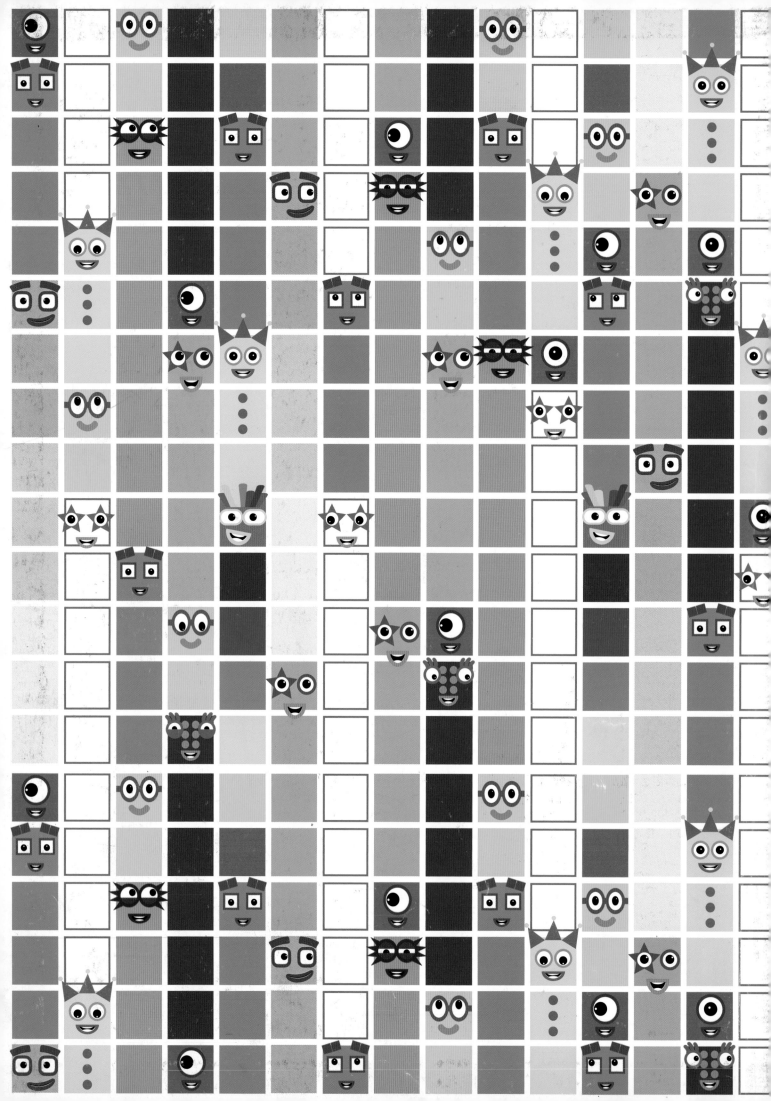